Pigasus: The Pig with wings

CHRISTOPHER BRICE

Illustrated by Pat Chatterley

ISBN: 978-1-5272-8696-2

DEDICATED TO

Farah & Thea - it is *always* OK to be yourself

ACKNOWLEDGMENTS

To the girls for the inspiration,

to JW for telling me "you're going to write a book",

to SE for the "wizardry",

to Mum & Dad for all of the word play jokes when I was a child,

and of course to H for the support. C

Once there was a magic land full of wondrous creatures,

they look just like normal animals but with slightly different features.

A unicorn is like a horse with a horn upon its head,

whereas a Pegasus is just like that,

but with great big wings instead.

A fairy is like a little girl, but with wings just like a bee,

this magic place was enchanted, as I hope that you can see.

There was one more, a pig with wings

her name was **Pigasus.**

The other animals weren't so sure,

"She's not one of us".

She tried frolicking with Pegasus, they wouldn't let her play,

"You must be mighty like a horse, and a Pegasus says "Neigh!""

She tried humming with the fairies, she was too big and dumpy, the mean looks from all the fairies made her truly grumpy.

She tried to swim with mermaids, but she couldn't flip and flap and bend,

She didn't like being different;

she went looking for

a new exciting friend.

She tried wallowing with some pigs;

she said "we look the same",

"We don't think that's quite right, but please join in our game".

So Pigasus played with her new friends, happy and full of fun,

but her wings were too big and strange and she went on the run.

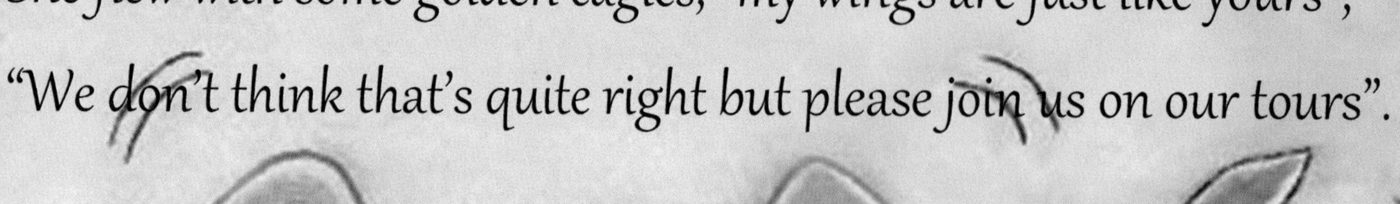

She flew with some golden eagles, "my wings are just like yours",

"We don't think that's quite right but please join us on our tours".

So Pigasus flew with her new friends, happy on her way,

but she could not soar high in the sky, and flew another way.

She joined a herd of elephants, “See, floppy ears and snouts”,

“We don’t think that’s quite right, but join our water fights and shouts”.

So Pigasus used her to snout to snort, a skill she could not hone,

She couldn't squirt water far enough and decided to go home.

"I wonder where Pigasus has gone, we all thought she was great,
It's a shame that we can't find her, she was the best of mates."

The animals went searching
for their friend,
“she must be so upset,
we love that she is different,
we are oh so glad we met”.

When they finally found her, they could see she had been crying,

"Please play with us, we'll have ice
cream", the elephant said, "I'm buying",

The animals were friends with Pigasus, and all were very glad,

So remember to be friendly when you can see someone is sad.

ABOUT THIS BOOK

Saturday morning drawing and colouring is a favourite in our house. A sketch of a pig with wings combined with childhood memories of Pegasus/pigasus jokes, a casual comment from a friend and "Pigasus: the pig with wings" was born.

ABOUT THE ILLUSTRATOR

Illustrated by Patricia Chatterley, who has humorously characterised, in watercolour the adventures of Pigasus, the pig with wings

www.patchatterley.com

Printed in Great Britain
by Amazon